Spookball
Champions

written and illustrated by
Scoular Anderson

PICTURE WINDOW BOOKS
Minneapolis, Minnesota

Managing Editor: Catherine Neitge
Story Consultant: Terry Flaherty
Page Production: Melissa Kes
Creative Director: Keith Griffin
Editorial Director: Carol Jones

First American edition published in 2006 by
Picture Window Books
5115 Excelsior Boulevard
Suite 232
Minneapolis, MN 55416
1-877-845-8392
www.picturewindowbooks.com

First published in Great Britain by
A & C Black Publishers Limited
37 Soho Square, London W1D 3QZ
Text and illustrations copyright © 2005 Scoular Anderson

Library of Congress Cataloging-in-Publication Data
Anderson, Scoular.
Spookball champions / written and illustrated by Scoular Anderson.
p. cm. — (Read-it! chapter books)
Summary: When Oliver spends the weekend with his aunt and uncle he soon
discovers the source of their sleepless nights.
ISBN 1-4048-1278-4 (hard cover)
[1. Haunted houses—Fiction. 2. Ghosts—Fiction.] I. Title. II. Series.
PZ7.A5495Spo 2005
[Fic]—dc22   2005007191

Table of Contents

Chapter One

Oliver's mom and dad were away for the weekend, so he was staying with Aunt Mona and Uncle Fred.

They lived in a big, old house on top of a hill. Oliver was sure it was haunted.

Aunt Mona and Uncle Fred were very dull. They had no children, no neighbors, no cats, and no dogs.

Aunt Mona moaned a lot.

All I do is go to the supermarket. The food in this house just vanishes!

Uncle Fred was very thin, so he didn't eat all the food. He just fretted a lot.

Oliver knew what was causing their problems.

Aunt Mona and Uncle Fred thought
Oliver was being silly.

After dinner, Oliver was allowed to watch
a program on TV with the sound
turned down.

The program was about some people who lived in a big house by the sea.
They turned it into a bed and breakfast.

That gave Oliver an idea.

Aunty, you could turn your house into a B & B...

... a haunted one as you've got a ghost!

11

Oliver couldn't get to sleep.
He waited for the ghost, but it didn't appear.

He jumped out of bed.

He opened his travel bag.
He was going to go
on a ghost hunt.

Chapter Two

Oliver had brought along some books
and games and
the ghost suit he had
worn at Halloween.
He pulled it on.

He crept out of his
room and along
the landing.

He went downstairs.

He went across the hall, then down some more stairs. He stopped at a door.

I think this is the kitchen.

He got ready to scare the ghost.

He pulled open the door.

It wasn't the kitchen.
It was a very untidy
closet.

Oliver pushed all
the stuff back.

He opened the next door. This was the kitchen, and there was a ghost—a fat ghost munching her way through a package of cookies.

The ghost threw a cookie at Oliver.

Oliver ducked and ran back upstairs.

He burst into Aunt and Uncle's
bedroom and got another surprise.
No wonder they didn't sleep well. There
was a thin ghost lying between them.

At that moment, Aunt Mona woke up.
The thin ghost disappeared.

Oliver pulled his ghost hat off.

Aunt and Uncle were more upset than they had been before.

Chapter Three

The next day,
Aunt Mona went
to the supermarket,
as usual.

Uncle Fred fretted about the squeaking
doors and spent all day oiling the hinges.

Oliver just waited for bedtime.
He wanted to go on another ghost hunt.

That night, Oliver waited until the house was quiet, then he got up. He pulled on his ghost suit again.

He went upstairs this time. He climbed right to the top of the house.

The last stairs were very narrow and led to the attic. Slowly, he opened the attic door. Sure enough, there was a ghost.

Septimus told Oliver why he didn't like them.

Oliver felt sorry
for Septimus.

He didn't reach the other ghosts, though.
He met Aunt Mona on the landing.

Chapter Four

Oliver just got back into bed when
he saw something move near the door.
It was Septimus.

30

Septimus took Oliver back up to the top of the house. Quietly, they opened the attic door.

Caesar was tossing his spookstick from
hand to hand.

Just then, Oliver remembered he had seen
something like that before.

He ran back downstairs. He pulled open
the closet next to the kitchen. All the
stuff fell out again.

They were difficult to catch and hold
because they were a little like ghosts.

Before Oliver went back to the attic, he
popped his head into the kitchen.

He peeked into Aunt and Uncle's bedroom.

He reached the attic again.

Septimus didn't look happy.

Septimus took a spookstick and crept into
the attic. The game of spookball was about
to begin.

Chapter Five

All at once, a spookball flew across the attic.
Caesar gave it a whack with his spookstick.

The ball zoomed down the attic and disappeared through the wall behind Septimus.

Caesar scored two more goals.

Another ball appeared.
Septimus was quicker
this time. He hit
it through the
wall behind
Caesar Snarl.

Just then, something made Oliver turn around.

Horatio and Serina were coming up the
stairs. They were holding spooksticks.

Horatio and Serina drifted past Oliver
and up into the attic.

Oliver ran to his bedroom and pulled on his ghost suit. He went back upstairs and found the spare spookstick.

The spookballs were very fast.

Oliver soon got the hang of it.

The house shook
for a whole hour.

Windows rattled.

CREAK!

BLAM!

Doors
slammed.

WHOOSH!

GROAN!

Curtains billowed.

ZIP!

SWISH!

Lights flickered
on and off.

BANG!

Then the spookballs stopped coming.
Sleepy Horatio had collapsed in a chair.
Serina was slumped in a corner. She had
eaten too many cookies.

Just as Septimus whacked
a ball past Caesar, the
clock down in the
hall struck midnight.

BONG! BONG! BONG!
BONG! BONG! BONG! BONG!
BONG! BONG! BONG! BONG!

Caesar, Horatio, and Serina were horrified.

A moment later, Caesar, Horatio, and Serina
vanished. Oliver saw them through a window,
drifting off down the hill. The house belonged
to Septimus once more.

Chapter Six

The next morning, Oliver got a surprise.
Aunt and Uncle were smiling.

Uncle had got up early and made a sign.

Of course, Oliver knew better than that …

Oliver's mom and dad came to pick him up.
Oliver promised to visit again soon. He was
looking forward to another game of spookball
in the attic.

About the author

Scoular Anderson is a popular author and illustrator. After studying graphic design at the Glasgow School of Art, he worked as an art teacher in Scotland.

Look for More
Read-It!
Chapter Books

Bricks for Breakfast by Julia Donaldson

Duncan and the Pirates by Peter Utton

Hetty the Yeti by Dee Shulman

The Mean Team from Mars by Scoular Anderson

Toby and His Old Tin Tub by Colin West

Looking for a specific title or level? A complete list
of *Read-it!* Chapter Books is available on our Web site:
www.picturewindowbooks.com